Agnes
and
Clarabelle
Celebrate!

 **READ & BLOOM BOOKS**

Agnes and Clarabelle
Agnes and Clarabelle Celebrate!

Stinky Spike the Pirate Dog
Stinky Spike and the Royal Rescue

Wallace and Grace Take the Case
Wallace and Grace and the Cupcake Caper

The Adventures of Caveboy
Caveboy Is Bored!

Agnes
and
Clarabelle
Celebrate!

Adele Griffin and Courtney Sheinmel
illustrated by Sara Palacios

BLOOMSBURY
NEW YORK   LONDON   OXFORD   NEW DELHI   SYDNEY

For Priscilla —A. G.
For Quinn —C. S.
To Eddie, my adventure mate and best friend —S. P.

Text copyright © 2017 by Adele Griffin and Courtney Sheinmel
Illustrations copyright © 2017 by Sara Palacios

First published in the United States of America in January 2017
by Bloomsbury Children's Books
www.bloomsbury.com

Bloomsbury is a registered trademark of Bloomsbury Publishing Plc

For information about permission to reproduce selections from this book, write to
Permissions, Bloomsbury Children's Books, 1385 Broadway, New York, New York 10018
Bloomsbury books may be purchased for business or promotional use. For information on bulk purchases
please contact Macmillan Corporate and Premium Sales Department at specialmarkets@macmillan.com

Library of Congress Cataloging-in-Publication Data
Names: Griffin, Adele, author. | Sheinmel, Courtney, author. | Palacios, Sara, illustrator.
Title: Agnes and Clarabelle celebrate! / by Adele Griffin and Courtney
Sheinmel ; illustrated by Sara Palacios.
Description: New York : Bloomsbury Children's Books, 2017.
Summary: Agnes and Clarabelle are best friends who love celebrating holidays together.
Identifiers: LCCN 2016022444 (print) • LCCN 2016030532 (e-book)
ISBN 978-1-61963-217-2 (hardcover)
ISBN 978-1-61963-218-9 (e-book) • ISBN 978-1-68119-094-5 (e-PDF)
Subjects: | CYAC: Best friends—Fiction. | Friendship—Fiction. | Holidays—Fiction. | BISAC:
JUVENILE FICTION / Readers / Chapter Books. | JUVENILE FICTION / Concepts / Seasons. |
JUVENILE FICTION / Animals / Farm Animals. | JUVENILE FICTION / Social Issues / Friendship.
Classification: LCC PZ7.G881325 Ak 2017 (print) • LCC PZ7.G881325 (e-book) | DDC [E]—dc23
LC record available at https://lccn.loc.gov/2016022444

Art created with colored pencil, watercolor, and digital tools
Typeset in Goudy Oldstyle and Cinderella • Book design by John Candell
Printed in China by C&C Offset Printing Co., Ltd., Shenzhen, Guangdong
1 3 5 7 9 10 8 6 4 2

Contents

Chapter 1
May Day

"Helllooo, Agnes! What a perfect day for the May Fair!" Clarabelle Chicken said.

"I hope you have fun," said Agnes Pig. "I am going to the library."

"But, Agnes," Clarabelle said, "look out the window—it's an outside day.

We can smell the cherry blossoms.
We can drink fresh-squeezed
lemonade. And the best part—this
year we are old enough to dance the
Maypole dance."

"The Maypole dance might make
me dizzy," said Agnes.

"Oh, Agnes, don't worry," said Clarabelle. "I'll help you. Besides, if you're not with me, it won't be half as fun."

"All right. I will try," said Agnes.

At the fair, Agnes and Clarabelle saw some of their other friends. Willa Goat rushed over with garlands of

cherry blossoms. "Happy May Fair!"
she called, placing one on each of
their heads.

"Thank you," said Agnes.

"Thank—*choo!*" squawked
Clarabelle.

"You're welcome," said Willa.
"The lemonade stand is over there!

I just squeezed my own cup! It's
delicious."

"Do you want some lemonade,
Clarabelle?" Agnes asked.

"Yes! I'm—*achoo*—coming,"
wheezed Clarabelle, "as soon as I

finish up these sneezes! *Achoo, achoo, achoo!*"

Agnes peered at her friend. "Clarabelle, your eyes are red and watery like when my aunt Petunia wears her Swine So Soft perfume.

6

Aunt Petunia is allergic to Swine
So Soft and you are allergic to those
flowers."

She whipped off Clarabelle's
garland. Clarabelle
stopped sneezing.

"I miss my
flowers already,"
she said. "Yours
look so pretty."

"Then I will take off my garland
too," said Agnes. "And we will be the
same."

7

"Thanks, Agnes! Let's go squeeze lemons!"

When they got to the lemonade stand, Agnes squeezed five lemons and added five teaspoons of sugar plus three ice cubes to her cup. She took a big gulp. "Ahh," she said. "This lemonade hits the spot."

Clarabelle squeezed
her lemon. No juice.
She squeezed harder.
No juice.

Clarabelle dropped
her lemon to the
ground and jumped
up and down on it.

Then she sat on
it. Not even a trickle.

"Agnes!" shouted
Clarabelle. "I am

9

so thirsty, but my lemon has gone dry!"

"We can share my lemonade," said Agnes.

"Agnes! Clarabelle!" Willa called. "Hurry, hurry! The music is starting for the Maypole dance. There won't be any streamers left!"

Agnes and Clarabelle ran to the Maypole.

Clarabelle felt shivery with delight. Every year since she was a tiny chick, she had watched the Maypole dance.

Now she was a big enough chicken to
dance in it herself.

Over and under, over and under—
"oops, sorry!" Clarabelle stumbled
smack into Katie Cow.

"Careful! This isn't a barnyard jig,
Clarabelle!" Katie mooed.

Clarabelle bent to pick up her dropped streamer and—*bonk!* "Watch it, Clarabelle!" snapped Jake Rabbit. "Sorry I stepped on your toe, but you're not supposed to just stop in the middle!"

By now the other dancers were passing her. Clarabelle's streamer was getting tangled. When she ran to catch up—*riiip.*

"Agnes!" squawked Clarabelle. "My streamer is ripped! I have to drop out of the Maypole dance."

But Agnes was dipping and rising
over and under, over and under.

There weren't any free chairs
so Clarabelle went and sat on her
lemon.

When the dance was over, Agnes hoofed it straight to Clarabelle.

"Did you see me, Clarabelle?" Agnes asked. "I danced the whole dance and I'm not dizzy at all. This May Day wasn't at all what I expected!"

Clarabelle thought about her sneezing, her hard lemon, her sore toe, and her ripped streamer. "It wasn't what I expected either. But I'm glad that you had a happy May Day. I wish I did too."

"That's why I have these streamers," Agnes said. "We can start practicing now so we'll both be ready to have lots of fun next year."

Chapter 2
Fourth of July

Agnes bounced out of bed. She
put on her marching-band hat and
picked up her baton from the floor.
She looked in the mirror and started
twirling. She took a break to eat
three PowerOink Energy bars. Then
she practiced some more.

19

"Wooooo!" Agnes tossed her baton into the air. Down it came, and she caught it perfectly.

On the way to the Firecracker Parade, she stopped at Clarabelle's house.

"Show me some twirls!" Clarabelle cried.

Agnes threw her baton up in the

air with her right hoof and caught it with her left.

Clarabelle cheered. "Wow! Piggy perfection!"

"I know," Agnes said. "I put my

snout to the grindstone and practiced
a lot. That's why Mayor Chirrup
picked me to lead his Fourth
of July float."

Together, they walked
to Main Street.

"Hi, Mr. Cow!"
Clarabelle clucked. "Hi, Rabbit
family! Hi, everyone in our whole
town!"

Agnes walked proud and tall and
waved to her friends.

"Everyone knows you are one of the most important pigs this day because of your hat," Clarabelle said. "Oooh, buttered corncobs!"

Clarabelle got a buttered corncob. Agnes used her bandana to shine her baton.

"Almost time for the parade to start," said Clarabelle. She flipped open her folding chair and settled in. "I'm in the front row, Agnes! I won't miss a single twirl!"

Agnes gave a hoofs-up and jumped on the float.

From up high, everything seemed different. Clarabelle looked smaller.

Uh-oh, thought Agnes. When she practiced, she had never thought about all these eyes on her.

Suddenly the float jerked forward.

Double uh-oh. Agnes had never thought about the float moving away from Clarabelle either.

"WELCOME TO OUR FOURTH OF JULY FIRECRACKER PARADE!" boomed Mayor Chirrup.

"Please give your biggest barnyard welcome to my lead baton twirler, AGNES PIG!"

Agnes had never thought about hearing her name boomed out of a megaphone.

She could feel her pink cheeks turning red. Her legs shook so hard she wanted to sit down.

But the band had started. Music blasted. The float was moving. The crowd was cheering.

"Agnes!" called Mayor Chirrup. "Say hello to your fans!"

But Agnes could not manage a single snort.

"Agnes, you can do it!" squawked Clarabelle. But her voice was fading fast.

"Clarabelle!" yelled Agnes, spinning around. "Wait! I can't hear you anymore! And I can barely see you! Somebody stop this float!"

But nobody was listening.

Nobody, except Clarabelle. In
a flurry of feathers, she flipped
aboard the float,
beak-first, and
hopped over to
Agnes.

31

"I'm here!" she said. "What's wrong? You were so excited for this parade!"

"Clarabelle, I'm scared," whispered Agnes. "This day is a lot bigger than I practiced for. Everyone is staring.

If I mess up, everyone will see—and laugh at me."

"No, they won't! But I have an idea. Let's pretend it's just us," said

Clarabelle. "I'm going to sit right here. And you twirl just for me." She shook her tail feathers and settled in.

Agnes stared at her friend. Then she smiled her

biggest, best parade-
day smile. She
picked up her
baton and threw
it in the air. She
twirled it like

no one was watching.

No one—except

Clarabelle.

Chapter 3
Halloween

"Halloween is the scariest night of the year," said Agnes.

"It's also the candy-est," said Clarabelle.

"The lucky thing is how we both like such different candy. So it's easy for us to trade," said Agnes.

"It's true!" said Clarabelle. "I like rainbow lollipops, gummy grubs, toasted-coconut marshmallow fluff drops, and chocolate-covered sunflower seeds."

"I like licorice twists," said Agnes. "And I also like sweet 'n' sour

seeds, mealy mints, choco-fleas, tutti-

frutti fruit stripe ribbons, and candy

corn!"said Clarabelle.

"I like licorice logs," said Agnes.

"But before candy comes costumes.

And I'm going to find the best one.
You know what that is?"

"What?" asked Agnes.

"A mean, green, warty old
witch with a pointy hat, a knobbly
broomstick, and a big black, swoopy
cape."

"That sounds scary," said Agnes.

"Spooky and scary," said Clarabelle.
"Are you going as a ghost again?"

"A ghost costume is too easy. I'm
going to be a toothbrush."

That night, Clarabelle pecked all around her house, searching for the things she needed to be the most terrifying Halloween witch.

In Granny Chicken's sewing basket, she found a wicked wig.

In her dad's dresser, she found a ghastly black cape.

There was goopy green witch skin in the bathroom.

And in the fridge lurked the
biggest, baddest wart a witch could
want.

In art class the next
day, Clarabelle put the
finishing touches on her
perfect, pointy witch hat. She set it
on her head and cackled. "How is

your toothbrush coming along, my pretty?"

"A toothbrush is too hard," said Agnes. "I'm going to be a flag."

The night before Halloween, Clarabelle called Agnes.

"This time tomorrow, I will be scaring the cobwebs out of our whole town. How's your flag costume coming along?"

"A flag is too hard. I'm going to be a windmill."

On Halloween night there was a
howling wind. The moon was full.
Bare branches scraped against the
windows.

"Ha-ha-ha, my pretties!" cackled
Clarabelle. "This witch will fly the
coop tonight!"

Clarabelle put on her wig. She tied her cape around her neck. She rubbed on her green witch skin and stuck a wart on her beak. She placed her pointy hat on top of her head. With one wing, she swept up her candy cauldron, and with the other, she grabbed her broom.

"Get ready to give up your candy for Clarabelle Witch!" She rushed to the mirror and—

EEEEEEEEEEEEEEEEE!

EEEEEEEEEEEEEEEE!
EEEEEEEEEEEEEEEEEEE!
EEEEEEEEEEEEEEEEEEE!

The doorbell rang. Clarabelle flew to open it.

"Wow, Clarabelle," said Agnes. "Great job! I hardly recognize you."

"Agnes, help! I've lost myself," Clarabelle wailed. "Clarabelle Witch looks too scary for Clarabelle Chicken!"

She pulled off her hat. "I don't want to be in this costume anymore. I don't want to be in a costume at all." She yanked off her wig and popped

off her wart. "I'm sorry if I ruined
Halloween."

"You haven't ruined anything," said
Agnes. "You don't need a big disguise.
You just need to be a little bit of
something else."

"Like what?" Clarabelle asked.

Agnes tapped her hooves together.
"I know," she said. "You can be a
chicken in a mustache."

"Ta-dah!"

"Happy Halloween!"

Chapter 4
New Year's Eve

Clarabelle walked into Agnes's house. "Happy New Year!" she squawked.

"Happy *Old* Year," said Agnes. "We have five hours and twenty-eight minutes left."

"Ten-nine-eight-seven-six-five-four-three-two-one!" Clarabelle

shouted. She blew on her noisemaker. "Look at how well I can count down now! Last year I forgot seven!"

"We have so much to do before the old year is over," said Agnes. "We need to measure ourselves. We need

to do our Tumble Terrific gymnastics dance. We need to share our favorite memories . . ."

"We need to tell our favorite jokes!" said Clarabelle.

"We need to sing our favorite songs!"

"And, most important, we have to—"

"MAKE OUR FAVORITE DRINK!" they yelled together.

"Hey, Agnes," Clarabelle clucked. "How do you make a dinosaur float?"

"How?" asked Agnes.

"First you scoop the ice cream. Then you pour the root beer. Then you add the dinosaurs!"

"Last float of the year is done," said Clarabelle. "What's next?"

"Now we measure ourselves," Agnes said.

"I grew one inch and three quarters longer!" cried Clarabelle.

"I grew four and a half inches . . . wider," said Agnes.

They performed their Tumble Terrific gymnastics dance.

"Let's make a tent," Clarabelle said.
"We can tell jokes and sing songs
inside it, so that it's extra-special."

"Good idea," said Agnes. She
pulled the chairs together.

Clarabelle stretched the sheet over
the backs.

"I love staying up late," said
Clarabelle. "Especially in a tent!"
Agnes set up her seven stuffed
animals inside the tent. "Mrs. Flea,
Rainbow Buttons, Tinker, Boo-Boo

Pig, Furryfeety,
King Oliver, and
Potholder, you
each get one last
kiss in the old
year," she said.

   "And one for Chester M.
Chicken," said Clarabelle.

   They kissed their stuffed animals.

                    Clarabelle yawned.

                    Agnes yawned too.

                    Clarabelle peeked

out of the tent. "Agnes," she whispered. "It is eight twenty-seven—twenty-seven minutes past our bedtime. Let's take a nap to make the new year come faster. "

Agnes looked worried. "What about our songs and our jokes?"

"How about we just close our eyes for three minutes?"

"Okay," said Agnes. "Wake me up in three minutes."

"Eeeeeeek!" Clarabelle hopped to her feet. "What is the sun doing in my eyes?"

Agnes jumped to her hooves and ran to the window. "What is the sun doing out there?!"

"Maybe because . . . it's eight thirty in the morning!?" cried Clarabelle.

Agnes ran to the window and pushed her snout against it. "Rotten corncobs! We're already in the new year and we never said good-bye to the old one!"

"Hooray!" Clarabelle blew on her kazoo. "No more waiting!" She threw a handful of confetti streamers.

Clarabelle nudged Agnes's elbow.
"Come on, Agnes. How about I make
us some New Year's Day waffles?"

Agnes shook her head.

"New Year's pancakes?" Clarabelle
asked.

"I'm not hungry for anything in the new year," said Agnes. "I'm sad. We let the old year down."

Clarabelle looked at her friend. "I know what," she said. "Let's go back into the tent."

"Why?" asked Agnes.

"Because if we put the flaps down, it will be dark. We can still pretend it is the old year. We can do the old year things we haven't done yet. We can sing and tell jokes and stories.

We can share memories—and for our
big finish, we can count down to the
brand-new year, and I will remember
seven!"

"Can we get flashlights too?" said

Agnes. "That will make it easier to pretend it's last night."

"Great idea, Agnes."

Clarabelle got the flashlights. Agnes found the list. Together, they went back into the tent. Clarabelle did not forget seven.

And then they went out into the very first morning of the new year.

READ & BLOOM

PLANT THE LOVE OF READING!

Agnes and Clarabelle are the best of friends!

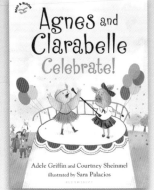

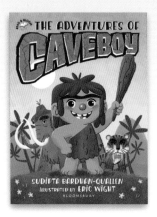

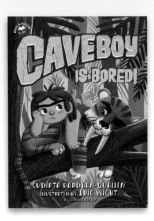

Caveboy is always ready for an adventure!

You don't want to miss these great characters! The Read & Bloom line is perfect for newly independent readers. These stories are fully illustrated and bursting with fun!

Stinky Spike can sniff his way out of any trouble!

Wallace and Grace are owl detectives who solve mysteries!

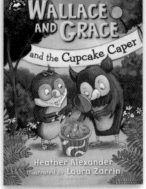

 www.bloomsbury.com • Twitter: BloomsburyKids • Facebook: KidsBloomsbury

Adele Griffin is the author of a number of acclaimed series books for young readers, including the Witch Twins, Vampire Island, and most recently, the Oodlethunks: *Oona Finds an Egg* and *Steg-O-Normous*. She lives in Brooklyn, New York, with her family and their very small dog, Edith.

www.adelegriffin.com

Courtney Sheinmel has written over a dozen highly celebrated books for kids and teens, including the Stella Batts series for young readers; the YA novel *Edgewater*; and a new middle-grade series, the Kindness Club. She lives in New York City.

www.courtneysheinmel.com

Sara Palacios is the illustrator of the Pura Belpré Honor–winning picture book *Marisol McDonald Doesn't Match* by Monica Brown. She lives in San Francisco and Mexico City.

www.sarapalaciosillustrations.com